# A Carousel Tale

Elisa Kleven

TRICYCLE PRESS
Berkeley

Ernst, a young blue crocodile, loved the carousel in the park. Every day he would say hello to the wooden animals. His favorite was the honey-colored dog.

"You always ride the dog," said Ernst's big brother Sol
one day. "Why do you like him so much?"

"His coat is sunny," said Ernst, "and his eyes are bright.
And his tail really wags."

"It's not wagging," said Sol. "It's just loose. The carousel
keeper should tighten it."

"I like the way it wags," said Ernst. He gave the dog a
hug, and the dog gave Ernst a ride, just like he always did.

Around and around they flew!

But the next day, when Ernst came to visit, the carousel was all covered up.

"Where are the animals?" Ernst asked the carousel keeper.

"They're safe inside that tent," she said, "snug and dry for winter. Don't worry, Ernst—you'll see your dog again in spring."

Ernst started for home, kicking an old scrap of wood as he went. After a few kicks, he saw that it wasn't just any old scrap: it was the dog's tail!

"What happened?" he asked. The tail just lay there, like a big wooden question mark.

Ernst hurried back to the carousel keeper. "Look! The dog lost his tail!"

"Oh, no," she said. "I must have knocked it off while I was working."

"Can you put it back on?" asked Ernst.

"Not now, I'm afraid. Everything's all sealed up."

"But the dog needs his tail!" said Ernst.

"I have an idea," said the carousel keeper. "Why don't you keep the tail until the weather warms up again? Then we'll put it back on the dog."

Ernst held the tail close. "I'll take good care of it," he promised.

"What have you got there, Ernst?" asked Sol, when Ernst arrived home.

"The carousel dog's tail," Ernst said. "It fell off. The carousel keeper said I could take care of it till spring."

"Wow! That's important," said Sol. "Lucky you."

But Ernst didn't feel so lucky. The tail made him feel sad.
It looked lonely without its dog. He set the tail on a shelf
with his toys. The tail looked lonelier than ever.

Ernst decided to cheer
it up. He gave the tail
bright eyes, a smile,

feathery wings,

and a big curly tail of its own.

How happy the tail looked now!

"Oooh!" said Sol, when he saw it. "Where did that pretty bird come from?"

"I made it," said Ernst, "out of the dog's tail."

"Ernst!" said Sol. "You were supposed to take care of the tail. And now you've covered it with paper and paint and—the tail isn't even yours!"

"It looked lonely," said Ernst. "I'll turn it back into a tail when the carousel opens up. I'll take off the feathers and wash off the paint."

"You'd better," said Sol.

Ernst patted his bird, glad that spring was a long way off.

That night, Ernst made the bird its
own little carousel.

And in the days to come, he did his best to keep it happy.

Together they played in the falling snow.

Together they flew through Ernst's dreams.

And after awhile, Ernst almost forgot that his bird had ever been a tail.

But one morning . . .

Ernst saw his old friend the dog flying around and around. And then he remembered.

"You're in trouble now," said Sol. "What are you going to do?"

Before Ernst could answer, the carousel keeper came over to greet him. "Hi Ernst, come on down! Your dog will be glad to see you again. Did you take good care of his tail?"

"I tried to," Ernst replied. "I think so. I'm not sure."

"Not sure?" asked the carousel keeper.

Ernst held out his bird. "I turned the tail into this."

"Ernst thought the tail looked lonely," said Sol.

"Oh my," said the carousel keeper. "My goodness."

"I can wash off the feathers and paint," offered Ernst.

The carousel keeper looked into the bird's bright eyes. She stroked its rainbow tail.

"You'll do no such thing," she said. "This is a wonderful bird you've made. As lovely as any carousel animal! Why don't you take it for a ride?"

"But the dog still needs his tail," said Ernst.

The carousel keeper nodded. "Yes, he does," she said. "I'll see what I can do."

"He's waited so long," said Ernst. "I'll see what I can do, too."

Ernst started for home, kicking along an old branch as he went. After a few kicks, he saw that it wasn't just any old branch. Ernst snatched it up, as if it were a puzzle piece and he knew just where it belonged.

"Look!" he cried, running back to the carousel keeper. "Look what I found!"

The carousel keeper laughed. "A tail! A perfect tail for the dog!"

Ernst and the carousel keeper
trimmed and sanded

and varnished the tail,

drilled a tiny hole in it,

and attached it to the dog—tight enough so that it wouldn't fall off, not so tight that it wouldn't wag.

Then together again, in the soft spring air,
they flew around and around.

For the Harris Family

ISBN 978-1-58246-239-4

Printed in China

*Library of Congress Cataloging-in-Publication Data*
Kleven, Elisa.
    A carousel tale / Elisa Kleven.
        p. cm.
    Summary: Given the responsibility of taking care of his favorite carousel
dog's tail during the winter, Ernst, the young blue crocodile, finds, as
time goes by, that he cannot resist his own artistic urges.
    ISBN-13: 978-1-58246-239-4 (hardcover)
    ISBN-10: 1-58246-239-9 (hardcover)
[1. Crocodiles—Fiction. 2. Merry-go-round—Fiction. 3. Tail—Fiction. 4.
Artists—Fiction.]  I. Title.
    PZ7.K6783875Car 2009
    [E]—dc22
                                                        2008011358

Design by Tasha Hall
Typeset in Bembo
The illustrations in this book were rendered in mixed media collage with
watercolors, ink, pastels, and colored pencils.

11 10 9 8 7 6 5 4 3 2

First Edition